HAM and PICKLES

First Day of School

written and illustrated by

Nicole Rubel

Harcourt, Inc.

Orlando   Austin   New York   San Diego   Toronto   London

Requests for permission to make copies of any part of the work should be mailed to the following address: Permissions Department, Harcourt, Inc., 6277 Sea Harbor Drive, Orlando, Florida 32887-6777.

www.HarcourtBooks.com

Library of Congress Cataloging-in-Publication Data
  Rubel, Nicole.
  Ham and Pickles: first day of school/Nicole Rubel.
  p. cm.
  Summary: Pickles is nervous about her first day of school, but taking advice from her big brother Ham may not be a good idea.
  [1. First day of school—Fiction. 2. Schools—Fiction.
  3. Brothers and sisters—Fiction.] I. Title.
  PZ7.R828Ham 2006
  [E]—dc22   2004018776
  ISBN-13: 978-0152-05039-9 ISBN-10: 0-15-205039-6

First edition
H G F E D C B A

Manufactured in China

The illustrations in this book were done on marker paper with black ink, markers, colored pencils, crayons, glitter, fabric paint, photographs, real flowers, rickrack, and beads.
The display type was set in EmmaScript and Potato Cut.
The text type was set in Potato Cut.
Color separations by Colourscan Co. Pte. Ltd., Singapore
Manufactured by SNP Leefung Holdings Limited
This book was printed on totally chlorine-free Stora Enso Matte paper.
Production supervision by Pascha Gerlinger
Designed by Scott Piehl and April Ward

To my husband,
Richard

Pickles was worried about starting school.

"What if my alarm doesn't ring and
I'm late?" she asked her brother, Ham.

"Never fear, I'll give you a jingle!" said Ham.

"I don't know what to wear," said Pickles. "The kids will make fun of me if I wear the outfit Grandma picked."

"Try my clothes and you'll fit right in," said Ham.

"What if the kids don't think I'm smart?" asked Pickles.

"Pickles, you're the brain in our family. Let's practice the alphabet one more time; it only has three letters," said Ham.

"What if I can't see over the other kids' heads?" asked Pickles.

"What do you think books are for?" asked Ham.

"What if I have the wrong school supplies?" asked Pickles.

"Follow me," said Ham. "This cooler
is filled with everything you'll need!"

"What do I do when I have to go
to the bathroom?" whispered Pickles.

"Jump like a kangaroo, leap like a frog, or hop like a grasshopper, and the teacher will excuse you," said Ham.

"I'm too nervous to eat breakfast," said Pickles.

"Relax," said Ham. "Open wide, toss in a handful of healthy cereal, and pour in milk."

"What if there's nowhere to sit
on the school bus?" asked Pickles.

"No problem," said Ham. "Throw one of these."

"How do I find my class?" asked Pickles.

"I'll draw you a map," said Ham.

"What if my teacher remembers you and
doesn't want me in her class?" asked Pickles.

"Wear this disguise," said Ham.

"No one is going to want to be my friend!" said Pickles.

"Sure they will," said Ham.

"Tell them, 'I'm so glad you **DON'T** have fleas!'"

"Do you have any other great ideas to ruin my day?"
cried Pickles. "And on top of that, I forgot my lunch!"

"Let's share," said Ham.

"Ham, you are a brother full of surprises!" said Pickles.
"Well, I'd say you learned a lot in school today," said Ham.

"Do you think you'll remember to take your lunch,
find your school supplies, and bring your map
so you don't get lost tomorrow?" Ham asked.

"Relax, Ham. I'll be just fine," said Pickles.